THE FESTIVAL OF INSIGNIFICANCE

MILAN KUNDERA

THE FESTIVAL OF
INSIGNIFICANCE

A NOVEL

Translated from the French by Linda Asher

HARPER

An Imprint of HarperCollins*Publishers*

HarperCollins books may be purchased for educational, business, or sales promotional use. For information, please e-mail the Special Markets Department at SPsales@ harpercollins.com.

Originally published as La fête de l'insignifiance *in France in 2014 by Gallimard.*

FIRST EDITION

Designed by Fritz Metsch

Library of Congress Cataloging-in-Publication Data
Kundera, Milan.
[Fête de l'insignifiance. *English*]
*The festival of insignificance : a novel / Milan Kundera;
translated from the French by Linda Asher.—First edition.*
pages   cm
ISBN 978-0-06-235689-5
I. Asher, Linda, translator. II. Title.
PQ2671.U47F4813   2015
843'914—dc23   015002938

15 16 17 18 19   OV/RRD   10 9 8 7 6 5 4 3

CONTENTS

PART ONE

Introducing the Heroes

Alain Meditates on the Navel

It was the month of June, the morning sun was emerging from the clouds, and Alain was walking slowly down a Paris street. He observed the young girls, who—every one of them—showed her naked navel between trousers belted very low and a T-shirt cut very short. He was captivated; captivated and even disturbed: It was as if their seductive power no longer resided in their thighs, their buttocks, or their breasts, but in that small round hole located in the center of the body.

This provoked him to reflect: If a man (or an era) sees the center of female seductive power in the thighs, how to describe and define the particularity of that erotic orientation? He improvised an answer: The length of the thighs is the metaphoric image of the long, fascinating road (which is why the thighs must be long) that leads to erotic achievement; indeed, Alain said to himself, even in midcoitus the length of the thighs endows woman with the romantic magic of the inaccessible.

If a man (or an era) sees the center of female seductive power in the buttocks, how to describe and define the particularity of that erotic orientation? He improvised an answer: brutality, high spirits, the shortest road to the goal; a goal all the more exciting for being double.

If a man (or an era) sees the center of female seductive power in the breasts, how to describe and define the particularity of that erotic orientation? He improvised an answer: sanctification of woman; the Virgin Mary suckling Jesus; the male sex on its knees before the noble mission of the female sex.

But how to define the eroticism of a man (or an era) that sees female seductive power as centered in the middle of the body, in the navel?

Ramon Strolls in the Luxembourg Gardens

At about the same time as Alain was musing on the different sources of feminine seductiveness, Ramon was approaching the museum at the edge of the Luxembourg Gardens, where for the past month Chagall paintings were on exhibit. He would have liked to see them, but he knew in advance that he would never have the stomach to willingly become part of that endless queue shuffling slowly toward the entrance. He looked at the people in line, their faces paralyzed by boredom, he pictured the galleries where their bodies and their chatter would obscure the paintings, and after a moment he turned away and started down a path that crossed the park.

There the atmosphere was more agreeable; the human species seemed fewer and freer; some were running, not because they were in a hurry but because they liked to run; some were sauntering along eating an ice cream; on the lawn among the trees the disciples of some Asian practice were performing strange slow motions; farther along, in an immense circle, stood great white statues of the queens of France; and farther still, on the grass beneath the trees, here and there in every direction, stood sculptures of poets, painters, scientists; Ramon stopped in front of a suntanned, appealing adolescent, naked under his shorts, who was selling masks of the faces of Balzac, Berlioz, Hugo, Dumas. Ramon could not help smiling, and he continued his walk through the garden of geniuses who, modest as they were, surrounded by the benign indifference of these strollers, must feel comfortably liberated, for no one stopped to examine their faces or read the inscriptions on the pedestals. Ramon inhaled that indifference like a soothing calm. Gradually a slow, almost happy smile appeared on his face.

At about the same time as Ramon was deciding against the Chagall show and choosing to stroll in the park, D'Ardelo was climbing the stairs to his doctor's office. It was exactly three weeks before his birthday. For several years past, he had come to detest birthdays. Because of the numbers affixed to them. Still, he did not quite reject them, for the pleasure of the attention paid him mattered more than the shame of aging. Especially because, this time, the medical appointment gave the approaching date a new coloration. For today he was to learn the results of all the tests that would tell him if his body's suspicious symptoms were due to cancer or not. He stepped into the waiting room and repeated to himself, in quaking tones, that in three weeks he would be marking both his so-distant birth and his so-near death—that he would be celebrating a double event.

But as soon as he saw the doctor's smiling face he understood that death had turned away. The doctor gripped his hand in brotherly fashion. D'Ardelo, his eyes tearing, could not speak a word.

The doctor's office was on l'avenue de l'Observatoire, a few hundred yards from the Luxembourg Gardens. D'Ardelo lived on a little street at the far side of the park, so he set out to return across it. Walking amid the greenery brought back a nearly giddy good humor, especially when he rounded the great ring of statues of the onetime queens of France, all of them carved from white marble, standing in solemn postures that struck him as humorous, even jolly, as if these women meant to cheer the good news he had just learned. Unable to help himself, he raised a hand in salute two or three times, and broke into laughter.

The Secret Charm of a Grave Illness

It was somewhere around there, close to the queens of France, that Ramon encountered D'Ardelo, who till a year earlier had been a colleague of his in an institute whose name does not matter here. The two men stopped face-to-face, and after the usual greetings, D'Ardelo started talking, his voice strangely excited:

"Listen, my friend—do you know La Franck, the great Madame Franck? Two days ago her partner died." He paused, and in Ramon's mind there appeared the face of a famous beauty he knew only from photographs.

"A very painful death," D'Ardelo continued. "She went through the whole thing with him. Ah, how she suffered!"

Fascinated, Ramon gazed at the cheerful face telling him this doleful story.

"But imagine—the very evening of the morning she'd held his dying body in her arms, she had dinner with a few friends and myself, and—you wouldn't believe it—she was almost merry! I was so impressed! What strength! What love of life! Her eyes were still red from tears, and here she was laughing! And yet we all knew how much she'd loved him! How she must have suffered! The power in the woman!"

Exactly as a quarter-hour earlier at the doctor's office, tears glistened in D'Ardelo's eyes. For as he spoke of Madame Franck's spirit, he was thinking of himself. Hadn't he also lived for a whole month in the presence of death? Hadn't his own character been put through a harsh ordeal as well? Even now that it was only a memory, the cancer stayed with him like the glow of a small bulb that, mysteriously, amazed him. But he managed to control his feelings and took a more prosaic tone: "By the way, if I'm not mistaken, don't you know some fellow who can put together a cocktail party—see to the food and all that?"

"I do, yes," said Ramon.

Said D'Ardelo, "I'm going to give a little party for my birthday."

After the excited remarks on the famous Madame Franck, the light tone of this last line allowed Ramon to smile: "I take it your own life is going well!"

Odd; the comment displeased D'Ardelo. As if the overly light tone destroyed the strange beauty of his good mood, magically marked as it was by the pathos of death, whose shadow still preoccupied him. "Yes," he said, "things are all right." Then after a pause he added, "Even though . . ."

He paused again, then: "You know, I'm just coming from my doctor."

The confusion on his interlocutor's face was gratifying; he let the silence go on, long enough so that Ramon could not help but ask: "And? Is something wrong?"

"There is."

And D'Ardelo fell silent again, and again Ramon could not help but ask: "What did the doctor tell you?"

At that moment D'Ardelo saw his own face in Ramon's eyes as if in a mirror: the face of a man already old but still good-looking, marked by a sadness that made it even more appealing; he thought how this sad handsome man was soon to celebrate his birthday, and the idea he had dwelled on before his doctor appointment sprang anew into his head—the enthralling idea of a double celebration, a celebration for birth and death at once. He went on watching himself in Ramon's eyes; then, in a very calm, very soft voice, he said, "Cancer."

Ramon stammered something, and clumsily, fraternally, he laid a hand on D'Ardelo's arm: "But that can be treated . . ."

"Too late, alas. But forget what I've just told you, don't mention it to anyone; and do give all the more thought to my cocktail party. Life must go on!" said D'Ardelo, and before resuming his walk, he raised a hand in a sign of farewell, and this diffident, nearly shy gesture had an unexpected charm that touched Ramon.

Inexplicable Lie, Inexplicable Laughter

The encounter of the two former colleagues ended with that beautiful gesture. But I cannot help wondering: Why did D'Ardelo lie?

D'Ardelo asked himself that question immediately afterward, and he did not know the answer either. No, he was not ashamed of having lied. What intrigued him was his inability to understand the reason for the lie. Normally, if a person lies, the point is to deceive someone and draw an advantage from that. But what could he possibly gain from inventing a case of cancer? Oddly, as he thought about the senselessness of his lie, he could not help laughing. And that laughter itself was incomprehensible to him. Why did he laugh? Did he find his behavior comical? No. A feel for the comical was actually not his strong point. Just simply, without knowing why, his fictional cancer pleased him. He went on his way and continued to laugh. He laughed and took pleasure in his good mood.

Ramon Pays Charles a Visit

An hour after his encounter with D'Ardelo, Ramon was already at Charles's apartment. "I come bearing a gift: a cocktail party job for you," he said.

"Bravo! We'll need it this year," said Charles, and he invited his friend to sit down across from him at a low table.

"A gift for you. And for Caliban. In fact, where is he?"

"Where should he be? At his house, with his wife."

"But I hope he's still doing cocktail parties with you?"

"Oh, yes. The theaters are still ignoring him."

Ramon saw a fairly thick book on the table. He leaned forward and could not hide his surprise: "*Memoirs of Nikita Khrushchev*. Why is that here?"

"Our master gave it to me as a gift."

"But what could he find interesting in it?"

"He underlined a few paragraphs for me. What I've read was quite amusing."

"Amusing?"

"The story of the twenty-four partridges."

"What?"

"The story of the twenty-four partridges. You don't know it? And yet that was the beginning of the great change in the world!"

"The great change in the world? Nothing less than that?"

"Nothing less. Caliban thinks so too. But tell me, what is this cocktail party, and at whose house?"

Ramon explained, and Charles asked, "Who is this D'Ardelo? A jackass like all my clients?"

"Of course."

"And what's his brand of stupidity?"

"What's his . . ." Ramon repeated, thoughtful. Then: "You know my friend Quaquelique?"

Ramon's Lesson on Brilliance and Insignificance

"My old friend Quaquelique," Ramon went on, "is one of the greatest womanizers I've ever known. Once I went to a reception where both of them were present, D'Ardelo and he. They didn't know each other. By chance they were standing in the same crowded room, and D'Ardelo probably never even noticed my

12

friend. There were some fine-looking women there, and D'Ardelo is crazy for them. He would go to impossible lengths to get them to pay attention to him. That night, witty talk shot from his mouth like fireworks."

"Off-color?"

"The contrary. Even his jokes are always moral, optimistic, respectable, but at the same time so elegantly subtle, convoluted, so difficult to understand, that they command attention but without an immediate effect. You have to wait three or four seconds until he breaks into laughter himself, and another few seconds go by before his listeners understand and politely join in. Then, just when everyone starts laughing—and this is a bit of technique I want you to appreciate!—he turns serious; neutral, almost indifferent, he watches his audience, and secretly, with a certain vanity, he takes delight in their laughter. Quaquelique's way is just the opposite. Not that he's silent: When he's in company he is constantly murmuring something under his breath, in his frail voice, more a kind of whistle than speech, but nothing he says draws any attention."

Charles laughed.

"Don't laugh. Speaking without drawing attention—that's not easy! Being ever-present by your voice and yet keeping unheard—that takes virtuosity."

"The point of that virtuosity escapes me."

"Silence draws attention. It can be disturbing. Make you seem enigmatic, or suspect. And that's precisely what Quaquelique wants to avoid. Like at that party I mentioned. There was a very beautiful woman there who fascinated D'Ardelo. Every now and then Quaquelique would make some completely banal remark to her, uninteresting, nothing. But the more agreeable to her in that it demanded no intelligent response whatever, no ready wit. After a while I notice that Quaquelique is no longer there. Intrigued now, I observe the woman. D'Ardelo has just uttered one of his bons mots, the five-second silence ensues, then he breaks into laughter, and after another three seconds the other people do the same. And meantime, under cover of the laughter, the woman has moved off toward the door. D'Ardelo, flattered by the echo his bon mot has set off, continues with his verbal display. A moment later he notices that the lovely woman is gone. And because he has no idea that a Quaquelique exists, he cannot comprehend her disappearance. He has understood nothing—and to this day he understands nothing—about the value of insignificance. And that is the answer to your question about the nature of D'Ardelo's stupidity."

"The uselessness of brilliance—yes, I get it."

"More than useless. It's harmful. When a brilliant fellow tries to seduce a woman, she has the sense she's entering a kind of competition. She feels obliged to shine too, to not give herself over without some resistance. Whereas insignificance sets her free. Spares her the need for vigilance. Requires no presence of mind. Makes her incautious, and thus more easily accessible. But to go on: With D'Ardelo, what you have is not an insignificant fellow but a Narcissus. And think about the precise meaning of that term: a Narcissus is not proud. A proud man has disdain for other people, he undervalues them. The Narcissus overvalues them, because in every person's eyes he sees his own image, and wants to embellish it. So he takes nice care of all his mirrors. And in the end that is what matters for the two of you: He is nice. Of course, in my opinion he is mainly a snob. But even between him and me, something has changed. I just learned that he's very sick. And from that moment on I see him differently."

"Sick? With what?"

"Cancer. I'm surprised to see how sad that's made me. He may be living out his final months." Then, after a pause: "I was touched by the way he told me about it—very laconic, shy even—no show of pathos, no narcissism. And suddenly, maybe for the first time, I felt a real sympathy for the jerk—a real sympathy."

PART TWO

The Marionette Theater

The Twenty-Four Partridges

After his long, wearing days, Stalin liked to linger awhile with his associates and relax by telling them little stories about his life. For example, this one:

One day he decides to go hunting. He puts on an old parka, clamps on skis, he takes a long shotgun and treks out thirteen kilometers. Then he sees before him a flock of partridges perched on a tree. He stops and he counts them. There are twenty-four of them. But what rotten luck—he's only brought along twelve shells! He fires, kills twelve birds, then turns around and treks the thirteen kilometers back to his house and picks up another dozen shells. Again he skis out the thirteen kilometers and reaches the partridges, who are still sitting on the same tree. And he finally kills them all . . .

"You like that?" Charles asks Caliban, who answers, laughing.

"If it was actually Stalin telling me that, I'd congratulate him! But where did you get that story?"

"Our master gave me this book, Khrushchev's *Memoirs*, published in France a very, very long time ago. In it Khrushchev reports the partridge story the way Stalin told it to their little group. But according to Khrushchev, nobody reacted the way you did. Nobody laughed. All of them, without exception, thought that what Stalin was telling them was nonsense, and they were disgusted by his lying. But they all kept silent, and only Khrushchev had the courage to tell Stalin what he thought. Listen to this!"

Charles opened the book and slowly read aloud: " 'What! You really mean to tell us that the partridges hadn't left their branch?' Khrushchev says.

" 'Exactly,' replies Stalin. 'They were still perched in the same spot.'

"But that's not the end of the story; you should know that at the end of the workday, all the men would go to the bathroom, a huge washroom that had the toilets in it as well. Imagine. On one wall a long row of urinals, on the facing wall a line of washbasins. Urinals in the shape of shells, in ceramic, all colors, decorated with flower motifs. Each member of Stalin's clan had his own urinal, created and signed by a different artist. None there for Stalin, though."

"And where did Stalin piss?"

"In a private stall at the other side of the building; and since he pissed all alone, never with his colleagues, all these fellows back in the bathroom were divinely free and finally dared to say out loud what they had to suppress in the chief's presence. Especially the day Stalin told them the story of the twenty-four partridges. I'll read you some more from Khrushchev: 'As we washed our hands, there in the bathroom, we were spitting with contempt: He was lying! He was lying! Not one of us doubted it.'"

"And who was he, this Khrushchev?"

"A few years after Stalin's death, he became the supreme leader of the Soviet empire."

After a pause, Caliban says: "The one thing I find unbelievable in that whole story is that nobody understood that Stalin was joking."

"Of course not," said Charles, and he laid the book back on the table. "Because nobody around him any longer knew what a joke is. And in my view, that's the beginning of a whole new period of history."

Charles Dreams of a Play for the Marionette Theater

In my unbeliever's dictionary, only one word is sacred: "friendship." The four friends I have introduced here—Alain, Ramon, Charles, and Caliban—I love. In my fondness for them, I brought Charles the Khrushchev book for them all to enjoy.

All four already knew the partridge story, including the magnificent finale among the toilets, when one day Caliban complained to Alain:

"I ran into your Madeleine, and I told her the partridge story. But to her it was just an incomprehensible anecdote about some hunter! Maybe the name 'Stalin' was vaguely familiar, but she didn't understand why a hunter would be called that."

"She's only twenty," Alain said quietly in defense of his girlfriend.

"If I'm calculating properly," Charles put in, "Madeleine was born about forty years after Stalin died. Myself, I had to wait about seventeen years after his death before I was born. And you, Ramon—when Stalin died . . ." He paused to work it out, then, a bit uncomfortable: "My God, you were already born!"

"I'm ashamed to say so, but it's true."

"Unless I'm mistaken," Charles went on, still to Ramon, "your grandfather and some other intellectuals signed a petition supporting Stalin, the great hero of progress."

"Yes," Ramon admitted.

"I imagine your father was already a little skeptical about him, your generation more so, and for mine, he had become the greatest criminal of all."

"Yes, that's how it goes," said Ramon. "People meet in the course of life, they talk together, they discuss, they quarrel, without realizing that they're talking to one another across a distance, each from an observation post standing in a different place in time."

After a moment Charles said: "Time moves on. Because of time, first we're alive—which is to say: indicted and convicted. Then we die, and for a few more years we live on in the people who knew us, but very soon there's another change; the dead become the old dead, no one remembers them any longer and they vanish into the void; only a few of them, very, very rare ones, leave their names behind in people's memories, but, lacking any authentic witness now, any actual recollection, they become marionettes. Friends, I am fascinated by that story Khrushchev tells in his memoirs. And I cannot shake off the urge to draw on it and invent a play for the marionette theater."

"The marionette theater? Don't you want to do it at the Comédie Française?" Caliban teased.

"No," said Charles, "because if that story about Stalin and Khrushchev were played by humans, it would be a lie. No one has the right to pretend to be reconstructing a human life that no longer exists. No one has the right to create a person from a marionette."

The Toilet Revolt

"They fascinate me, those people around Stalin," Charles went on. "I imagine them shouting out their

23

revolt there among the toilets! They'd all longed so much for the right moment, when they could finally say aloud all they were thinking. But there was one thing they never suspected: Stalin was watching them and waiting for that moment with the same impatience as theirs! The moment when his whole gang would go off to the toilets was delectable for him as well! My friends, I can just see him! Very quietly, on tiptoe, he slips down a long corridor, sets his ear against the door to the toilet room, and listens. Those Politburo heroes, shouting and stomping around inside, cursing him, and him, he's hearing them and he's laughing. 'He lied, he lied!' Khrushchev howls, his voice thunders, and Stalin, with his ear pressed to the door—oh, I can see him, I can see him, Stalin savoring his comrade's moral outrage—he's guffawing like a madman, and he doesn't even try to muffle the great sound of his laughter, because the people in the toilets are howling like madmen too, and they can't hear him over their own racket."

"Yes, you already told us about that," says Alain.

"Yes, I know, but the most important thing, the real reason Stalin liked to repeat himself and kept telling the same story of the twenty-four partridges over and over to that same little audience—that, I haven't told you yet. And that's what I see as the main plot of my play."

"And what was the reason?"

"Kalinin."

"What?" Caliban asked.

"Kalinin."

"Never heard the name."

Though a little younger than Caliban, Alain was better read, and he knew: "That must be the fellow they renamed a famous German city after, the city where Immanuel Kant lived his whole life and that's called 'Kaliningrad' now."

Just then, from the street, a horn sounded, loud, impatient.

"I must leave you," Alain said. "Madeleine is waiting for me. Till next time!"

Madeleine was waiting for him in the street on a motorbike. It was Alain's bike, but they shared it.

The Next Time They Meet, Charles Gives His Friends a Lecture on Kalinin and the Capital of Prussia

"Since its founding, the illustrious Prussian city was called Königsberg, which means 'the king's mountain.' Only after the last war did it become Kaliningrad. 'Grad' means 'city' in Russian. Thus: Kalinin City. The century we just had the luck to survive was crazy about renaming things. Tsaritsyn was renamed Stalingrad, then Stalingrad became Volgograd. Saint

Petersburg became Petrograd, then Petrograd was re-named Leningrad, and eventually Leningrad became Saint Petersburg. Chemnitz became Karl-Marx-Stadt and Karl-Marx-Stadt went back to Chemnitz again. Königsberg was called Kaliningrad—but wait: Kaliningrad remained and will forever remain unrenameable. Kalinin's fame will outlast everyone else's."

"But who was he?" Caliban asked.

"A man," Charles went on, "with no real power, a poor innocent puppet who nonetheless was for a long time the president of the Supreme Soviet, thus from the standpoint of protocol the highest representative of the state. I've seen his picture: an old militant worker with a pointed goatee, in a badly cut jacket. Now, Kalinin was already an old man, and his swollen prostate very often forced him to go piss. The urinary urge was always so abrupt and so strong that he would have to run to a urinal even during an official luncheon, or in the middle of some speech he himself might be delivering to a big audience. He had got very adept at handling the problem. To this day all of Russia recalls a great ceremony to inaugurate an opera house in some city in Ukraine, during which Kalinin was giving a long, solemn speech. He had to break off every two minutes and, each time, as he left the rostrum, the orchestra would strike up some folk music, and lovely blond Ukrainian ballerinas would leap onto the stage and begin dancing. Each time he returned to the dais,

Kalinin was greeted with great applause; when he left again, the applause was still louder, to greet the advent of the blond ballerinas—and as his goings and comings grew more frequent, the applause grew longer and stronger, more heartfelt, so that the official celebration was transformed into a joyful mad orgiastic riot whose like the Soviet state had never seen or known.

"But alas, between times, when Kalinin was back in the little group of his comrades, no one was interested in applauding his urine. Stalin would recite his anecdotes, and Kalinin was too disciplined to gather the courage to annoy him by his goings and comings from the toilet. The more so since, as he talked, Stalin would fix his gaze on Kalinin's face growing paler and paler and tensing into a grimace. That would incite Stalin to slow his storytelling further, to insert new descriptions and digressions, and to drag out the climax till suddenly the contorted face before him would relax, the grimace vanished, the expression grew calm, and the head was wreathed in an aureole of peace; only then, knowing that Kalinin had once again lost his great struggle, Stalin would move swiftly to the denouement, rise from the table and, with a bright, friendly smile, bring the meeting to an end. All the other men would stand too, and stare cruelly at their comrade, who positioned himself behind the table, or behind a chair, to hide his wet trousers."

Charles's friends were delighted to picture the scene,

and only after a pause did Caliban break into the amused silence: "Still, that doesn't explain at all why Stalin gave the poor prostatic's name to the German city that was the lifelong home of the famous . . . the famous . . ."

"Immanuel Kant," Alain whispered to him.

Alain Uncovers Stalin's Ill-Understood Affection

When Alain met with his friends a week later, in some bistro (or at Charles's place, I don't recall), he immediately broke into their conversation:

"I'd like to say that for me it's not at all puzzling that Stalin would put Kalinin's name to Kant's illustrious city. I don't know what reasons you might have come up with yourselves, but for my part I see only one: Stalin felt an enormous affection for Kalinin."

The happy surprise on his friends' faces pleased and even inspired him: "I know, I know—the word 'affection' doesn't fit with Stalin's reputation—he's the Lucifer of the century, I know; his life was filled with plots and conspiracies, betrayals, wars, jailings, murders, massacres. I don't deny that; on the contrary, I'd even emphasize it, to make absolutely clear that with that enormous load of cruelty he must have undergone, committed, and lived through, it would be impossible for him to muster an equally enormous amount of compassion. That would be beyond human capacity! To live the life he lived, he would have had to first anesthetize, then totally suppress any faculty for compassion. But as he looked at Kalinin, in those brief intervals away from the massacres, in those quiet moments of restful talk, it all changed: He was confronted with a completely different pain—a small, concrete, individual, comprehensible pain. He looked at his suffering comrade, and, to his own mild astonishment, he felt stirring a faint, modest emotion that was almost unfamiliar, or anyhow forgotten: love for a man who is suffering. In his ferocious life, this moment was a kind of respite. The fondness grew in Stalin's heart at the same rate as the pressure of urine in Kalinin's bladder. The rediscovery of an emotion he had long ceased to feel struck him as an unspeakable beauty.

"And that," Alain continued, "is what I see as the only possible explanation for the curious renaming of Königsberg as Kaliningrad. It occurred thirty years before I was born, and yet I can imagine the situation: With the war over, the Russians annex a famous German city to their empire, and they must Russify it with a new name. And not just any name! This rebaptism must draw on a name famous over the entire planet, a name whose brilliance will silence enemies! The Russians have plenty of such names: Catherine the Great! Pushkin! Tchaikovsky! Tolstoy! Not to mention the generals who had conquered Hitler and who at the time were adulated everywhere! So how are we to understand why Stalin would choose the name of such a nonentity? That he would make such an obviously idiotic decision? Only private, secret reasons can explain that. And we know what they are: He feels affection for the man who has suffered for his sake, before his very eyes, and he wants to thank him for his loyalty, honor him for his devotion. Unless I'm mistaken—Ramon, you can set me straight!—for that brief moment in history, Stalin is the most powerful statesman in the world, and he knows it. He feels a mischievous delight at being, among all the presidents and kings, the only one who can scorn the gravity of grand, cynically calculated political gestures, the only one who can allow himself to make some thoroughly personal decision, a decision that's capricious, unreasonable, splendidly bizarre, gorgeously absurd."

On the table stood an open bottle of red wine. Alain's glass was already empty; he refilled it and went on: "Now, telling the story before you all, I see a deeper and deeper meaning in it." He swallowed a mouthful, then again went on: "To suffer to keep from soiling your shorts . . . To be a martyr to your personal hygiene . . . To struggle against urine as it stirs, as it swells, threatens, attacks, kills . . . Is there any heroism that's more prosaic, more human? To hell with the so-called great men whose names adorn our streets. They all became famous through their ambitions, their vanity, their lies, their cruelty. Kalinin is the only one whose name will live on in memory of an ordeal that every human being has experienced, in memory of a desperate battle that brought misery on no one but himself."

He ended his speech, and all were moved.

After a silence, Ramon said: "You are absolutely right, Alain. After I die, I intend to wake up every ten years to check whether Kaliningrad is still Kaliningrad. As long as that is the case, I'll feel a little solidarity with humankind, reconciled with it, and can go back down into my tomb."

PART THREE

Alain and Charles Often Think About Their Mothers

The First Time He Was Gripped by the Navel's Mystery
Was When He Saw His Mother for the Last Time

Returning slowly to the house, Alain observed the girls, who—every one of them—showed her naked navel between trousers belted very low and a T-shirt cut very short. As if their seductive power no longer resided in their thighs, their buttocks, or their breasts, but in that small round hole located in the center of the body.

Do I repeat myself? Am I starting this chapter with the same words I used at the very beginning of this novel? I know. But even if I've already described Alain's passion for the enigma of the navel, I do not want to hide the fact that this enigma does preoccupy him still, the way you yourselves are preoccupied for months, if not years, by similar problems (certainly far more pointless than the one obsessing Alain). So: Ambling along the streets, he would often think about the navel, untroubled at repeating himself and even strangely obstinate about doing so, for the navel woke in him a distant memory: the memory of his last encounter with his mother.

He was ten at the time. He and his father were alone on vacation in a rented villa with a garden and a swimming pool. It was the first time she had come to their house, after an absence of several years. They closed themselves into the villa, she and her former husband. For miles around the atmosphere was stifling from it. How long did she stay? Probably not more than an hour or two, during which time Alain tried to entertain himself in the pool. He had just climbed out when she paused there to say her good-byes. She was alone. What did they say to each other? He doesn't know. He only remembers that she was sitting on a garden chair and that he, in his still-wet bathing trunks, stood facing her. What they said is forgotten, but one moment is fixed in his memory, a concrete moment, sharply etched: Seated in her chair, she looked intensely at her son's navel. He still feels that gaze on his belly. A gaze that is difficult to understand; it seemed to him to express an inexplicable mix of compassion and contempt; the mother's lips had taken the shape of a smile (a smile of compassion and contempt together); then, without rising from the chair she leaned toward him and, with her index finger, touched his navel. Immediately afterward she stood up, kissed him (Did she really kiss him? Probably, but he is not sure), and was gone. He never saw her again.

A small car moves along the road beside a river. The chilly morning air makes even more forlorn the charmless terrain, somewhere between the end of a suburb and open country, there where houses grow scarce and no pedestrians are to be seen. The car stops at the side of the road; a woman gets out— young, rather beautiful. A strange thing: She pushes the door shut so negligently that the car must not be locked. What is the meaning of that negligence, so unlikely these days, with thieves about? Is the woman so distracted?

No, she doesn't seem distracted; on the contrary, determination is visible on her face. This woman knows what she wants. This woman is pure will. She walks some hundred yards along the road toward a bridge over the river, a rather high, narrow bridge forbidden to vehicles. She steps onto it and heads toward the far bank. Several times she looks around her, not like a woman expected by someone, but to be sure there is no one expecting her. Midway across the bridge she stops. At first glance she appears to be hesitating, but, no, it's not hesitation or a sudden flagging of determination; on the contrary, it's a pause to sharpen her concentration, make her will steelier yet. Her will? To be more precise: her hatred. Yes, the pause that looked like hesitation is actually an appeal to her hatred to stand by her, to support her, not to desert her for an instant.

She lifts a leg over the railing and flings herself into the void. At the end of her fall, she slams brutally against the hardness of the water's surface and is paralyzed by the cold, but after a few long seconds she lifts her face, and, since she is a good swimmer, all her automatic responses surge forward against her will to die. She plunges her head under again, forces herself to inhale water, block her breathing. Suddenly she hears a shout. A shout from the far bank. Someone has seen her. She understands that dying will not be easy and that her greatest enemy will be not her good-swimmer's irrepressible reflex but a person she had not figured on. She will have to fight. Fight to rescue her death.

She Kills

She looks over toward the shout. Someone has leaped into the river. She considers: Who will be quicker: she, in her resolve to stay underwater, to take in water, to drown herself; or he, the oncoming figure? When she is half-drowned, with water in her lungs and thus weakened, won't she be all the easier prey for her savior? He will pull her toward the bank, lay her out on the ground, force the water out of her lungs, apply mouth-to-mouth, call the rescue squad, the police, and she will be saved and ridiculed forevermore.

"Stop! Stop!" the man shouts.

Everything has changed. Instead of diving down beneath the water, she raises her head and breathes deeply to collect her strength. He is already in front of her. It's a young fellow, a teenager who hopes to be famous, have his picture in the papers, he just keeps repeating: "Stop! Stop!" He's already reaching a hand toward her, and she, rather than evading it, grasps it, grips it tight, and pulls it (and him) down toward the depths of the river. Again he cries, "Stop!" as if it is the only word he can speak. But he will not speak it again; she holds on to his arm, draws him toward the bottom, then stretches the whole length of her body along the boy's back to keep his head underwater. He fights back, he thrashes, he has already taken in water, he tries to strike the woman, but she stays lying firmly on him; he can no longer lift his head to get air, and after several long, very long, seconds, he ceases to move. She holds him like that for a while longer; it is as if, exhausted and trembling, she is resting, laid out along him; then, convinced that the man beneath her will not stir again, she lets go of him and turns away toward the riverbank she came from, so as not to preserve within her even the shadow of what has just occurred.

But what's going on? Has she forgotten her resolve? Why does she not drown herself, since the person who tried to rob her of her death is no longer alive? Why, now that she is free, does she no longer seek to die?

Life unexpectedly recovered has been a kind of shock that broke her determination; she no longer has the strength to concentrate her energy on dying; she is shaking; suddenly stripped of any will, any vigor, mechanically she swims toward the place where she abandoned the car.

She Returns to the House

Little by little she feels the water grow less deep, she touches her feet to the riverbed, she stands; she loses her shoes in the mud and hasn't the strength to search for them; she leaves the water barefoot and climbs the bank to the road.

The rediscovered world has an inhospitable appearance, and suddenly anxiety seizes her: She hasn't got the car key! Where is it? Her skirt has no pockets.

Heading for your death, you don't worry about what you've dropped along the way. When she left the car, the future no longer existed. She had nothing to hide. Whereas now, suddenly, she has to hide everything. Leave no trace. Her anxiety grows stronger and stronger: Where is the key? How to get home?

She reaches the car, she pulls at the door and, to her astonishment, it opens. The key awaits her, abandoned on the dashboard. She sits at the wheel and sets her naked feet on the pedals. She is still shaking. Now she is shaking with the cold as well. Her shirt, her skirt, are drenched with dirty river water running everywhere. She turns the key and drives off.

The person who tried to impose life on her has died from drowning, and the person she was trying to kill in her belly is still alive. The idea of suicide is ruled out forever. No repeats. The young man is dead, the fetus is alive, and she will do all she can to keep anyone from discovering what has happened. She is shaking, and her will revives; she thinks of nothing but her immediate future: How to get out of the car without being seen? How to slip unnoticed, in her dripping dress, past the concierge's window?

Alain felt a violent blow on his shoulder.

"Watch out, you idiot!"

He turned and saw a girl passing him on the sidewalk with a rapid, energetic stride.

"Sorry!" he cried after her (in his frail voice).

"Asshole!" she answered (in her strong voice) without turning around.

The Apologizers

Alone in his studio apartment, Alain noticed that he was still feeling pain in his shoulder, and he decided that the young woman who had jostled him in the street so effectively, the night before last, must have done it on purpose. He could not forget her strident voice calling him "idiot" and he heard again his own supplicating "Sorry!" followed by the answering "Asshole!" Once again he had apologized over nothing! Why always this stupid reflex of begging pardon? The memory would not leave him, and he felt he had to talk with someone. He phoned Madeleine. She wasn't in Paris, and her cell phone was off. So he punched in Charles's number, and no sooner did he hear his friend's voice than he apologized, "Don't be angry. I'm in a very bad mood. I need to talk."

"It's a good moment. I'm in a foul mood too. But why are you?"

"Because I'm angry with myself. Why is it that I find every opportunity to feel guilty?"

"That's not so awful."

"Feeling guilty or not feeling guilty—I think that's the whole issue. Life is a struggle of all against all. It's a known fact. But how does that struggle work in a society that's more or less civilized? People can't just attack each other the minute they see them. So instead they try to cast the shame of culpability on the other. The one who manages to make the other one guilty will win. The one who confesses his crime will lose. You're walking along the street, lost in thought. Along comes a girl, walking straight ahead as if she were the only person in the world, looking neither left nor right. You jostle one another. And there it is, the moment of truth: Who's going to bawl out the other person, and who's going to apologize? It's a classic situation: Actually, each of them is both the jostled and the jostler. And yet some people always—immediately, spontaneously—consider themselves the jostlers, thus in the wrong. And others always—immediately, spontaneously—consider themselves the jostled ones, therefore in the right, quick to accuse the other and get him punished. What about you—in that situation, would you apologize or accuse?"

"Me, I'd certainly apologize."

"Ah, my poor friend, so you, too, belong to the army of apologizers. You expect to mollify the other person by your apologies."

"Absolutely."

"And you're wrong. The person who apologizes is

declaring himself guilty. And if you declare yourself guilty, you encourage the other to go on insulting you, blaming you, publicly, unto death. Such are the inevitable consequences of the first apology."

"That's true. One should not apologize. And yet I prefer a world where people would all apologize— everybody, without exception, pointlessly, excessively, for nothing at all, where they'd load themselves down with apologies—"

"You say that in such a sad voice," said Alain in surprise.

"For the past two hours I've been thinking of nothing but my mother."

"What's happening?"

Angels

"She's sick. I'm afraid it may be serious. She just phoned me."

"From Tarbes?"

"Yes."

"Is she alone there?"

"Her brother lives in the house with her. But he's even older than she is. I'd like to get into the car right now and go there, but it's impossible. I have a job this evening that I can't cancel. A really stupid job. But to-morrow I'll go."

"It's odd—I often think about your mother."

"You'd like her. She's funny. She already has trouble walking, but we have a really amusing time together."

"Do you get your love of clowning from her?"

"Maybe."

"It's strange."

"Why?"

"From what you've always told me, I imagined her like a figure out of a Francis Jammes poem. Surrounded by suffering animals and aged peasants. Amid donkeys and angels."

"Yes," said Charles, "she is like that." Then, after a few seconds: "Why did you say angels?"

"Why does that surprise you?"

"In my play—" He stopped for a moment, then: "You understand, my play for marionettes, it's just a game, a crazy idea, I'm not writing it, I'm just imagining it, but what can I do if there's nothing else that interests me? . . . Anyway, in the last act of this play, I imagine an angel."

"An angel? Why?"

"I don't know."

"And how will the play end?"

"For the moment all I know is that at the end there'll be an angel."

"What does that mean to you, an angel?"

"I don't know much about theology. I imagine an angel mainly from what people say to someone they want to thank for their goodness—'You're an angel.' People often say it to my mother. That's why I was surprised when you said you pictured her surrounded by donkeys and angels. That's how she is."

"I don't know much theology either. I just remember that there are angels that are thrown out of heaven."

"Yes. Angels thrown out of heaven."

"Besides that, what else do we know about angels? That they're slender . . ."

"True, it's hard to imagine an angel with a big belly."

"And that they have wings. And that they're white. White. Listen, Charles, unless I'm mistaken, angels have no sex. That may be the key to their whiteness."

"Could be."

"And to their goodness."

"Could be."

Then after a silence, Alain said: "Does an angel have a navel?"

"Why?"

"If an angel has no sex, he's not born from a woman's belly."

"Certainly not."

"So he would be without a navel."

"Yes, no navel, for sure . . ."

Alain thought about the young woman who, beside the swimming pool of a vacation house, had touched her index finger to the navel of her ten-year-old son, and he said to Charles, "It's strange. Me too, for a while now, I keep picturing my mother . . . in all kinds of possible and impossible situations—"

"All right now, friend, let's stop there! I've got to get ready for this damn cocktail party."

PART FOUR

They Are All in Search
of a Good Mood

Caliban

In his first occupation, which at the time he saw as his life purpose, Caliban was an actor; that was the profession registered in black and white on his identity papers, and now it was as an actor with no bookings that he had been drawing unemployment benefits for a long while. The last time he was seen on a stage, he was playing Caliban the savage in Shakespeare's *The Tempest*. His skin smeared with brown makeup, a black wig on his head, he howled and capered about like a madman. His performance had so delighted his friends that they decided to call him by the name that would remind them of it.

That was already a long time ago. Since then, theaters had not cared to hire him, and his benefits diminished year after year, as indeed they did for thousands of other unemployed actors, dancers, singers. Then Charles, who earned his living by managing social events for private clients, took him on as a waiter. Caliban could thus make a little money, but besides, still an actor seeking to regain his lost mission, he also saw the work as an occasion to shift identities from time to time. His aesthetic ideas were a little naive (wasn't his patron saint, Shakespeare's Caliban, naive too?), and he believed that an actor's feat was the more remarkable the further the character was from his actual life. With this in mind, he insisted on working with Charles not as a Frenchman but as a foreigner who spoke only a language no one around him would understand. When he had to pick a new homeland, perhaps because of his somewhat swarthy skin tone, he chose Pakistan. Why not? Choosing a homeland—nothing easier. But inventing its language, that is difficult.

As an improvisation, try talking in a fictional language for even thirty seconds! You'll keep repeating the same sounds time and again, and your babble will be instantly unmasked as a sham. Inventing a nonexistent language requires giving it some acoustical credibility: creating a particular phonetics and never pronouncing an *a* or an *o* as the French do; deciding on which syllable the stress will regularly fall. It is also recommended, for a natural sound, to devise an underlying grammar for these meaningless sounds, and to determine which word is to be a verb and which a noun. And when the game involves a pair of friends, it is important to work out the role of the second person, the Frenchman—in this case, Charles; though he does not speak this Pakistani, he must know at least a few words of it so that in an emergency the two can communicate without using a word of French.

That had been difficult but entertaining. Alas, even the most entertaining prank cannot evade the law of growing stale. The two friends enjoyed the game for the first few parties, but rather soon Caliban began to feel that all that laborious masquerading served little purpose, for the guests showed no interest in him and, what with his incomprehensible language, did not listen to him, settling for simple gestures to indicate what they wanted to eat or drink. He had become an actor without an audience.

White Jackets and the Portuguese Girl

They reached D'Ardelo's apartment two hours before the party was to begin.

"Madame, this is my assistant. He is Pakistani. I'm sorry, but he doesn't speak a word of French," said Charles, and Caliban bowed ceremoniously before Madame D'Ardelo and uttered a few incomprehensible phrases. Madame D'Ardelo's rather blasé indifference, with no attention to the information, confirmed Caliban's sense of the pointlessness of his laboriously invented language, and he began to feel a touch of melancholy.

Fortunately, immediately following this disappointment, a small pleasure consoled him: The maid whom Madame D'Ardelo had ordered to make herself useful to the two waiters could not take her eyes off so exotic a creature. She spoke to Caliban several times, and when she came to understand that he knew only his own language, she was at first disconcerted and then strangely relaxed. For she was Portuguese. Since Caliban spoke to her in Pakistani, she had a rare chance to drop French, a language she disliked, and to use only her own native tongue, like him. Their communication in two languages neither understood brought them close.

A small van stopped in front of the building and two drivers brought up all the provisions Charles had ordered—bottles of wine and whiskey, ham, sausages, pastries—and set them down in the kitchen. With the maid's help, Charles and Caliban covered a long table set up in the salon with an enormous cloth and set out plates, platters, glasses, and bottles. Then, as the cocktail hour drew near, they retired to a small room Madame D'Ardelo had assigned them. From a valise, they lifted out two white jackets and slipped them on. They needed no mirror, they simply looked each other over and could not suppress a little laugh. This always gave them a brief instant of pleasure. They almost forgot that they were working out of necessity, to earn a living; seeing themselves in their white costumes, they had the sense they were doing it for fun.

Then Charles went off to the salon, leaving Caliban to arrange the remaining platters. A very young girl, self-assured, stepped into the kitchen and turned to the maid: "You are not to show yourself out front in the salon for even a second! If our guests saw you they'd run right out!" Then, examining the Portuguese girl's lips, she exploded with laughter: "Where did you dig up that lipstick? You look like some African bird! A parrot from Bourenbouboubou!" and she left the kitchen, laughing.

Her eyes moist, the Portuguese girl told Caliban (in Portuguese): "Madame is nice! But her daughter! She's just so mean! She said that because she likes you! When there are men around she's always mean to me! She loves humiliating me in front of men!"

Unable to respond, Caliban stroked her hair. She raised her eyes and said (in French): "Look at me, is my lipstick so ugly?" She turned her head right and left so he could inspect the full span of her lips.

"No," he said (in Pakistani), "your lipstick color is a very good choice."

In his white jacket, the maid found Caliban even more sublime, even more unbelievable, and she told him (in Portuguese): "I'm so glad you are here."

And he, carried away by his own eloquence, said

(still in Pakistani): "And not just your lips, but your face, your body, all of you—just as I see you here before me; you're lovely, very lovely—"

"Oh, I'm so glad you're here!" the maid responded (in Portuguese).

The Photo on the Wall

Not only for Caliban, who no longer finds anything amusing in his masquerade, but for all my characters, that evening is clouded with sadness: for Charles, who had confessed to Alain his fears for his ailing mother; for Alain, moved by that filial love that he himself had never experienced, and moved as well by the image of an old countrywoman who belonged to a world unknown to him but for which he felt nostalgia all the more. Unfortunately, when he'd hoped to prolong the phone conversation, Charles was already late and had had to hang up. Alain then picked up his cell phone to call Madeleine again. But hers rang and rang; in vain. As he often did in similar instances, he turned his attention to a photo hanging on his wall. There was no other photo in his studio but that one—the face of a young woman: his mother.

A few months after Alain's birth, she had left her

husband, who, given his discreet ways, had never spoken ill of her. He was a subtle, gentle man. The child did not understand how a woman could abandon a man so subtle and gentle, and understood even less how she could have abandoned her son, who was also (as he was aware) since childhood (if not since his conception) a subtle, gentle person.

"Where does she live?" he had asked his father.

"Probably in America."

"What do you mean, 'probably'?"

"I don't know her address."

"But it's her duty to give it to you."

"She has no duty to me."

"But to me? She doesn't want to hear news of me? She doesn't want to know what I'm doing? She doesn't want to know that I think about her?"

One day the father lost control:

"Since you insist, I'll tell you: Your mother never wanted you to be born. She never wanted you to be around here, to be burying yourself in that easy chair where you're so comfortable. She wanted nothing to do with you. So now you understand?"

The father was not an aggressive man. But despite his great reserve, he had not managed to hide his profound disagreement with a woman who had tried to keep a human being from coming into the world.

I have already described Alain's last encounter with his mother, beside the swimming pool of a rented vacation house. He was ten at the time. He was sixteen when his father died. A few days after the funeral, he had torn his mother's photograph out of a family album, got it framed, and hung it on his wall. Why was there no picture of his father in his apartment? I don't know. Is that illogical? Certainly. Unfair? Without a doubt. But that's how it is: On the walls of his studio there hung only a single photograph: the one of his mother. With which, from time to time, he would talk:

How to Give Birth to an Apologizer

"Why didn't you have an abortion? Did he stop you?"

A voice came to him from the photograph:

"You'll never know that. Everything you imagine about me is just fairy tales. But I love your fairy tales. Even when you made me out to be a murderer who drowned a young man in the river. I liked it all. Keep it up, Alain. Tell me a story! Go on, imagine! I'm listening."

And Alain imagined. He imagined the father on his mother's body. Before their coitus, she warned him: "I didn't take the Pill, be careful!" He reassured her. So she makes love without mistrust; then, when she sees the signs of climax appear on the man's face, and grow, she starts to cry out: "Watch out!" then "No! No! I don't want to! I don't want to!" but the man's face is redder and redder, red and repugnant; she pushes at the heavier weight of this body clamping her against him, she fights, but he wraps her still tighter, and she suddenly understands that for him this is not the blindness of passion but will—cold, premeditated will—while for her it is more than will, it is hatred, a hatred all the more ferocious because the battle is lost.

This was not the first time Alain imagined their coitus; this coitus hypnotized him and caused him to suppose that every human being was the exact replica of the instant during which it was conceived. He stood at his mirror and examined his face for traces of the double, simultaneous hatreds that had led to his birth: the man's hatred and the woman's hatred at the moment of the man's orgasm; the hatred of the gentle and physically strong coupled with the hatred of the courageous and physically weak.

And he thinks how the fruit of that double hatred could only be an apologizer. He was gentle and intelligent like his father; and he would always remain an intruder, as his mother had viewed him. A person who is both an intruder and gentle is condemned, by an implacable logic, to apologize throughout his whole life.

He looked at the face hung on the wall and once again he saw the woman who, defeated, in her dripping dress, climbs into the car, slips unnoticed past the concierge's window, climbs the staircase, and, barefoot, returns to the apartment where she will stay until the intruder leaves her body. And where, a few months later, she will abandon the two of them.

Ramon Arrives at the Cocktail Party in a Foul Mood

Despite the compassion he had felt at the end of their encounter in the Luxembourg Gardens, Ramon could not change the fact that D'Ardelo belonged to the sort of people he did not like. Even though they had a trait in common—the passion for dazzling others; for startling them by an amusing remark; for conquering a woman before their very eyes. Except that Ramon was not a Narcissus. He enjoyed success but feared to rouse envy; he liked being admired but fled the admirers. His diffidence had turned into a love of solitude after he sustained a few wounds in his private life, but especially since the previous year, when he had been obliged to join the dismal army of the retired: His nonconformist remarks, which had used to keep him young, now despite his misleading appearance made him an uncontemporary character, a person not of our time, and thus old.

So he decided to boycott the cocktail party he'd been invited to by his former colleague (a man not yet retired), and he did not change his mind until the last minute, when Charles and Caliban swore that only his presence would make bearable their ever more boring task as waiters. Still, he arrived very late, long after a guest had delivered a speech in the host's honor. The apartment was jammed. Knowing no one, Ramon headed for the long table behind which his two friends were serving drinks. To lighten his foul mood, he greeted them with a few words in rough imitation of their Pakistani babble. Caliban replied in his authentic version of the same babble.

Then, with a wineglass in hand, still in a foul mood, wandering among the strangers, Ramon was drawn to the excitement of a few people turned toward the vestibule door. A woman appeared there, slender and beautiful, in her fifties. Her head tilted back, she slid a hand several times beneath her hair, lifting it, then letting it fall back gracefully, and she turned to offer everyone the voluptuously tragic expression of her face; no one among the guests had ever met her, but all knew her from photos: the famous Madame Franck. She stopped at the long table, bent over, and with grave concentration indicated to Caliban various canapés she liked.

Her plate was soon full, and Ramon thought of what D'Ardelo had told him in the Luxembourg Gardens: She had just lost her partner whom she had loved so passionately that, through some magical decree from the heavens, her sadness at the moment of his death had been transubstantiated into euphoria, and that her lust for life had grown a hundredfold. He watched her: She put canapés into her mouth, and her face displayed the vigorous motions of mastication.

When D'Ardelo's daughter (Ramon knew her by sight) noticed the tall, famous woman, the girl's mouth stopped moving (she, too, was masticating something) and her legs started running: "Darling!" She tried to embrace La Franck, but the woman was holding a plate at stomach level that thwarted her.

"Darling!" the girl repeated as La Franck's mouth worked over a great mass of bread and salami. Unable to swallow the whole thing, she deployed her tongue to push the mouthful into the space between molars and cheek; then, with some effort, she tried to say a few words to the girl, who could not make them out.

Ramon took a couple of steps forward to observe them from close up. The D'Ardelo girl swallowed what she had in her own mouth, and declared in ringing tones: "I know everything, oh, I know everything! But we will never allow you to be alone! Never!"

La Franck, her gaze set emptily ahead (Ramon could see that she had no idea who this person was), moved a segment of the mass into the middle of her mouth, chewed it, swallowed half of it, and said: "Human existence is nothing but solitude."

"Oh, how true that is!" cried the D'Ardelo girl.

"A solitude surrounded by other solitudes," La Franck added, then she swallowed down the rest, turned, and moved away.

Ramon was unaware that a light smile of amusement was forming on his face.

Alain Sets a Bottle of Armagnac on Top of His Armoire

At about the same moment as that unexpected little smile was brightening Ramon's face, a telephone ring interrupted Alain's musings on the genesis of an apologizer. He knew instantly that it was Madeleine. Difficult to understand how these two could always talk for so long and with such pleasure, when they had so few interests in common. When Ramon had described his theory about observation posts standing each on a different point in history, from which people talk together unable to understand one another, Alain had immediately thought of his girlfriend, because, thanks to her, he knew that even the dialogue between true lovers, if their birth dates are too far apart, is only the intertwining of two monologues, each holding for the other much that is not understood. That was why, for instance, he never knew if the reason Madeleine twisted the names of famous men of the past was that she had never heard of them or that she was parodying them on purpose, to make clear to everyone that she was not the least bit interested in anything that had happened before her own lifetime. Alain was not troubled by this. It amused him to be with her just as she was, and he could be all the more content afterward when he was back in the solitude of his own studio, where he had hung poster reproductions of paintings by Bosch, Gauguin (and who knows who else) that marked out his own private world for him.

He always had a vague idea that if he had been born some sixty years earlier he would have been an artist. A truly vague idea, since he did not know what the word "artist" meant nowadays. A painter turned window dresser? A poet? Is there still such a thing as a poet? What gave him most pleasure, these past few weeks, was sharing in Charles's fantasy, his marionette play, in this nonsense that delighted him precisely because it made no sense.

Knowing full well that he could not earn a living doing what he would have liked to do (but did he know what he would like to do?), he had chosen, after university, a job in which he was forced to make use not of his originality, his ideas, his talents, but only of his intelligence—that is to say, of that mathematically measurable ability that distinguishes among individuals only quantitatively—one person having more, the other less of it, Alain rather more, such that he had been well paid and could occasionally buy himself a bottle of Armagnac. A few days earlier he had bought a bottle when he noticed on its label a vintage year that matched the date of his own birth. He had thus promised himself he would open it on his birthday to celebrate his greatness with his friends, the greatness of this very great poet who, out of his humble veneration of poetry, had vowed never to write a single line.

Content and almost jolly after his long chat with Madeleine, he climbed onto a chair with the bottle of Armagnac and set it on top of a high, very high, armoire. Then he sat on the floor and, leaning against the wall, fixed on it a gaze that slowly transfigured it into a queen.

Quaquelique's Call to a Good Mood

While Alain was gazing at the bottle atop the armoire, Ramon went on scolding himself for being somewhere he did not want to be; all these people displeased him, and he was especially intent on avoiding D'Ardelo; suddenly he saw the man just a few yards away, standing before La Franck, whom he was trying to captivate with his eloquence; to get away from them, Ramon took refuge once again at the long table where Caliban was busy pouring Bordeaux into the glasses of three guests; through his gestures and grimaces, he was giving them to understand that the wine was of rare quality. Knowing the proper behavior, the gentlemen picked up their glasses, warmed them for a long moment between their palms, took a sip and held it in their mouths, displayed to one another their faces, expressing first intense concentration, then amazed admiration, and finished by loud proclamations of delight. The whole thing lasted barely a minute, until this festival of tasting was harshly interrupted by their conversation, and Ramon, watching them, had the sense that he was attending a funeral where three gravediggers were burying the sublime taste of the wine by tossing onto its coffin the earth and the dust of their chatter; again a smile of amusement formed on his face, while just then a very frail voice, barely audible, more whistle than speech, sounded behind his back: "Ramon! What are you doing here?"

He turned. "Quaquelique! What are *you* doing here?"

"Looking for a new girlfriend," he answered, and his deeply uninteresting little face beamed.

"My dear fellow," said Ramon, "you're the same as always."

"You know, boredom—there's nothing worse.

That's why I keep changing girlfriends. Without that, no good mood for me!"

"Ah, good moods!" exclaimed Ramon, as if enlightened by those two words. "Yes, you said it! A good mood—that's what it's all about, exactly! Ah, what a pleasure to see you! A few days ago, I was talking about you to my friends. Oh, Quaqui, my Quaqui, I've got a lot to tell you—"

Just then he spotted, a few steps away, the pretty face of a young woman he knew; this fascinated him; it was as if these two chance encounters, magically bound by the same moment in time, shot him through with energy; in his head the echo of the words "good mood" resonated like a call to arms.

"Excuse me," he said to Quaquelique, "we'll talk later—you understand—"

Quaquelique smiled. "Of course I understand. Go on, go!"

"I'm very happy to see you again, Julie," Ramon told the young woman. "It's ages since I've run into you."

"That's your fault," the young woman replied, looking him impudently in the eyes.

"Until this minute I had no idea what unreasonable reason brought me to this dreadful party. Now I know."

"And suddenly the dreadful party is no longer dreadful." Julie laughed.

"You've de-dreaded it," Ramon said, laughing too. "But why are you here?"

She nodded toward a group gathered around an old (very old) university celebrity. "He's always got something to say." Then with a promising smile: "I'm eager to see you later this evening . . ."

In an excellent mood, Ramon glimpsed Charles behind the long table, looking oddly absent, his gaze set high above him. The strange stance intrigued Ramon; then he said to himself: "What a pleasure not to worry about something happening up there, what a pleasure to be right down here," and he watched Julie walking away: The motion of her behind was both a greeting and an invitation.

PART FIVE

A Little Feather Floats
Beneath the Ceiling

A Little Feather Floats Beneath the Ceiling

" . . . Charles . . . oddly absent, his gaze set high above him. . . ." These are the words I wrote in the last paragraph of the previous chapter. But what was he looking at up there?

A tiny thing fluttering beneath the ceiling; a very small white feather that slowly hovered, floated downward, then upward. Behind the long table covered with platters, bottles, and glasses, Charles stood motionless, his head slightly tilted back, while one after another the guests, intrigued by his stance, began to follow his gaze.

Watching the little feather's wanderings, Charles felt a stab of anguish: It struck him that the angel he had thought about these past weeks was alerting him that it was already somewhere here, very nearby. Perhaps, frightened, before it was to be flung out of heaven it had let loose from its wing this tiny barely visible feather, like a wisp of its anxiety, like a memory of the happy life it had shared with the stars, like a calling card meant to explain its arrival and declare the approaching end.

But Charles was not yet ready to face the end; he would have liked to put it off for later. The image of his ailing mother rose up before him, and his heart clenched.

Still, the feather was there; it rose and fell, while at the far side of the salon Madame Franck was also looking up toward the ceiling. She raised a hand with the index finger outstretched, offering the feather a place to land. But the feather avoided La Franck's finger and went on its wandering way.

The End of a Daydream

Above La Franck's left hand, the feather continued to wander, and I imagine some twenty men who, gathered around a long table, focus their own gaze upward, though no feather is floating there; they are all the more uncertain and nervous because the thing they fear stands neither before them (like an enemy that could be killed), nor beneath them (like a snare the secret police could thwart), but somewhere above them, like a threat, an invisible, incorporeal, incomprehensible, ungraspable, unpunishable, mischievously mysterious threat. A few of them rise from their seats without knowing where they mean to go.

I see Stalin, impassive, seated at the end of the long table, growling: "Calm down, you cowards! What are you afraid of?" Then, in a louder voice: "Sit down, the meeting is not over!"

At the window Molotov murmurs: "Joseph, something is brewing. There's talk they're going to knock down your statues." Then, under Stalin's mocking gaze, under the weight of his silence, he docilely lowers his head and goes back to sit down at the table.

When all of them have returned to their places, Stalin says, "That's called the end of a daydream! All daydreams come to an end. It's always as unexpected as it is inevitable. Don't you know that, you morons?"

All the men keep silent—except Kalinin, who is incapable of controlling himself and proclaims loudly: "Whatever happens, Kaliningrad will always be Kaliningrad!"

"For good reason! And I am very pleased to know that Kant's name will forever be bound to yours," Stalin answers, increasingly amused. "Because, you know, Kant fully deserves it." And his laugh, at once forlorn and gay, roams the big room for a long while.

The distant echo of Stalin's laughter trembles faintly in the salon. From behind the long drinks table, Charles continued to watch the little feather above La Franck's raised index finger, and Ramon, amid all those upturned heads, was overjoyed that the moment had come when, unobserved and very discreetly, he could slip away with Julie. He looked left and right, but she was not there. He could still hear her voice, her parting words that rang like an invitation. He could still see her magnificent behind as it moved away, sending him greetings. Perhaps she'd gone off to the bathroom? To freshen her makeup? He stepped into a small hallway and waited outside the door. Several women came out, looked at him suspiciously, but she did not appear. It was all too clear. She was already gone. She had turned him down. Instantly all he wanted was to quit this dreary gathering, abandon it immediately, and he headed for the door. But a few steps before he reached it, Caliban appeared before him carrying a platter: "Good God, Ramon, you're so sad! Quick, take a whiskey."

How do you refuse a friend? And besides, their sudden encounter had an irresistible advantage: Since all the halfwits around them were staring as if hypnotized at the ceiling, toward the same absurd spot, he could finally be alone with Caliban, here below, on the ground, in utter privacy, as if on an island of freedom. They stood still, and Caliban, to say something cheery, made a remark in Pakistani.

Ramon answered (in French): "I congratulate you, my friend, on your superb linguistic performance. But instead of cheering me up, you're sending me deeper into my misery."

He took a whiskey from the tray, swallowed it, set the glass down, took another, and held on to it: "Charles and you invented this Pakistani-language farce to entertain yourselves during these fashionable cocktail parties where you're just the poor lackeys of the snobs. The pleasure of a hoax was supposed to protect you. In fact, that's always been our strategy. We've known for a long time that it was no longer possible to overturn this world, nor reshape it, nor head off its dangerous headlong rush. There's been only one possible resistance: to not take it seriously. But I think our jokes have lost their power. You force yourself to speak Pakistani to cheer yourself up. In vain. All you get out of it is weariness and boredom."

He stopped for a moment, and saw that Caliban had laid a finger on his lips. "What is it?"

Caliban tilted his head toward a man—small, bald—a few yards from them, the only person whose gaze was locked not onto the ceiling, but onto the two of them.

"So what?" asked Ramon.

"Don't speak French! He's listening to us," Caliban whispered.

"But why does that disturb you?"

"Please, not in French! For the past hour I've had the feeling he's watching me."

Seeing his friend really upset, Ramon said a few nonsense words in Pakistani.

Caliban did not react; then, somewhat calmer: "He's looking away now," he said, and then: "He's leaving."

Uneasy, Ramon drank up his whiskey, set the empty glass back onto the tray, and mechanically picked up another (the third by now). Then, his tone serious: "I swear, I had never even imagined that possibility. But, yes, you're right! If some servant to truth should discover that you're French! Then of course you'll be suspect! He'll think you must have some shady reason to be hiding your identity! He'll alert the police! You'll be interrogated! You'll explain that your Pakistani character was a joke. They'll laugh at you: What a stupid alibi! You must certainly have been up to no good! They'll put you in handcuffs!"

He saw the anxiety return to Caliban's face.

"Ah no, no! Forget what I just said! I'm talking nonsense. I'm exaggerating!" Then, lowering his voice, he added: "Still, I know what you mean. Joking has become dangerous. My God, you must know that!

Remember the story about the partridges that Stalin used to tell his pals. And remember Khrushchev, shouting in the lavatory! Khrushchev, the great hero of truth, spluttering with contempt! That scene was prophetic! It really was the start of a new era. The twilight of joking! The post-joke age!"

Once again a little cloud of sorrow passed above Ramon's head, as for a moment he pictured Julie and her behind moving away; he quickly emptied his glass, set it down, took another (the fourth), and proclaimed, "My dear friend, I lack only one thing—a good mood."

Caliban looked around him again; the little bald man was gone; that calmed him down. He smiled.

And Ramon went on: "Ah, a good mood! You've never read Hegel? Of course not. You don't even know who he is. But our master who invented us once made me study him. In his essay on the comical, Hegel says that true humor is inconceivable without an infinite good mood—listen, that's exactly what he says: 'infinite good mood, *unendliche Wohlgemutheit*.' Not teasing, not satire, not sarcasm. Only from the heights of an infinite good mood can you observe below you the eternal stupidity of men, and laugh over it."

Then, after a moment, glass in hand, he said slowly: "But how can we achieve it, this good mood?" He drank, and set the empty glass on the tray. Caliban smiled a farewell, turned, and left. Ramon raised his arm toward the departing friend and called: "How can we achieve that good mood?"

Madame Franck Departs

The only reply Ramon heard was shouting, laughter, applause. He turned to look at the far end of the salon, where the little feather had finally alighted on the upright finger of La Franck, who raised her hand as high as possible, like an orchestra conductor directing the final bars of a great symphony.

Then the excited crowd slowly calmed down, and La Franck, her hand still high, declaimed in clarion tones (despite the morsel of cake still in her mouth): "Heaven has sent me a sign that my life is going to be even more glorious than before. Life is stronger than death, because life is nourished by death!"

She fell silent, looked at her audience, and swallowed the last bits of pastry. The people around her applauded, and D'Ardelo approached her as if to embrace her solemnly in the name of all the assembly. But she did not see him and, her hand still raised up toward the ceiling, the little feather caught between thumb and index, slowly, with dancing steps, skipping slightly, she moved toward the exit.

Ramon Departs

In wonderment Ramon gazed upon the scene and felt that laughter reborn in his body. What—laughter? Could it be that the Hegelian good mood had at last noticed him from on high and decided to welcome him to her home? Could this be a mandate to take hold of that laughter and keep it close as long as possible?

His furtive glance fell upon D'Ardelo. Throughout the whole evening he'd managed to avoid him. Should he, out of politeness, go and bid the man good-bye? No! He would not spoil his great unique moment of good humor! Best to leave as quickly as he could.

Elated and completely drunk, he ran down the stairway, out to the street, and looked for a cab. Now and then a shout of laughter burst from him.

Eve's Tree

Ramon was looking for a taxi, and Alain was sitting on the floor of his studio, leaning against the wall, his head bent low: Perhaps he had dozed off?

A female voice woke him.

"I like everything you've said to me so far, I like everything you're inventing, and I have nothing to add. Except, maybe, about the navel. To your mind, the model of a navel-less woman is an angel. For me, it's Eve, the first woman. She was not born out of a belly but out of a whim, the Creator's whim. It's from her vulva, the vulva of a navel-less woman, that the first umbilical cord emerged. If I'm to believe the Bible, other cords too: with a little man or a little woman attached to each cord. Men's bodies were left with no continuation, completely useless, whereas from out of the sexual organ of every woman there came another cord, with another woman or man at the end of each one, and all of that, millions and millions of times over, turned into an enormous tree, a tree formed from the infinity of bodies, a tree whose branches reached to the sky. Imagine! That gigantic tree is rooted in the vulva of one little woman, of the first woman, of poor navel-less Eve.

"For me, when I got pregnant, I saw myself as a part of that tree, dangling from one of its cords, and you, not yet born—I imagined you floating in the void, hooked to the cord coming out of my body, and from then on I dreamed of an assassin way down below, slashing the throat of the navel-less woman, I imagined her body in death throes, decomposing, so that whole enormous tree that grew out of her—suddenly without roots, without a base—starts to fall, I saw the infinite spread of its branches come down like a gigantic rainfall, and—understand me—what I was dreaming of wasn't the end of human history, the abolition of any future; no, no, what I wanted was the total disappearance of mankind together with its future and its past, with its beginning and its end, along with the whole span of its existence, with all its memory, with Nero and Napoleon, with Buddha and Jesus; I wanted the total annihilation of the tree that was rooted in the little navel-less belly of some stupid first woman who didn't know what she was doing and what horrors we'd pay for her miserable coitus, which had certainly not given her the slightest pleasure."

The mother's voice went silent, Ramon stopped a cab, and Alain, leaning against the wall, dozed off again.

PART SIX

Angels Falling

Farewell to Mariana

With the last guests gone, Charles and Caliban put the white jackets back in their valise and became ordinary beings. Saddened, the Portuguese girl helped them to clear the plates, the crockery, the bottles, and to set everything in a corner of the kitchen for the catering staff to carry away the next day. With every intention of being useful to them, she kept close by them, so that the two friends, too weary to go on spouting ridiculous insane words, could not get a single second's rest, not a single moment to exchange a sensible idea in French.

Stripped of his white jacket, Caliban looked to the Portuguese woman like a god come down to earth and become a mere man, someone a poor servant girl could easily talk to.

"You really don't understand anything I say?" she asked him (in French).

Caliban answered something (in Pakistani) very slowly, carefully enunciating each syllable, looking deep into her eyes.

She listened attentively as if, pronounced at a lesser pace, this language could become more comprehensible to her. But she had to acknowledge her defeat. "Even if you speak slowly, I don't understand a thing," she said, sadly. Then, to Charles: "Can you tell him something in his language?"

"Only very simple phrases, things about cooking."

"I know," she sighed.

"You like him?" Charles asked.

"Yes," she said, blushing hard.

"What can I do for you? Should I tell him you like him?"

"No," she replied, with a violent shake of her head. "Tell him . . . tell him . . ." She stopped to think: "Tell him that he probably feels very lonely here, in France. Very lonely. I wanted to tell him, if he needs anything, any help, or even if he needs to eat . . . that I could . . ."

"What's your name?"

"Mariana."

"Mariana, you're an angel. An angel appearing in the midst of my journey."

"I'm not an angel."

Suddenly uneasy, Charles agreed: "I hope not, too. Because it's only toward the end that I see an angel. And the end—I'd like to put that off as long as possible."

Thinking of his mother, he forgot what Mariana

had asked him; he remembered it only when she reminded him, in a supplicating tone: "I asked you, monsieur, to tell him—"

"Oh, yes," Charles said, and he said a few nonsense sounds to Caliban.

His friend moved toward the Portuguese girl. He kissed her on the mouth, but the girl held her lips closed tight, and their kiss was intransigently chaste. Then she ran off.

That modesty made the two men nostalgic. In silence they went down the stairs and took their seats in the car.

"Caliban! Wake up! She's not for you!"

"I know that, but let me regret it. She's all goodness, and I'd like to do something good for her, too."

"But there's nothing good you can do for her. Just by your presence you can only do her harm," Charles said, and he started the car.

"I know. But I can't help it. She makes me nostalgic for chastity."

"What? For chastity?"

"Yes. Despite my stupid reputation as an unfaithful husband, I have an insatiable nostalgia for chastity!" And he added: "Let's stop by Alain's place."

"He's asleep by now."

"So we'll wake him up. I feel like drinking. With you and him. Raise a glass to the glory of chastity."

A long, aggressive horn sounded from the street. Alain opened the window. Down below, Caliban slammed the car door and shouted, "It's us! Can we come up?"

"Yes, sure! Come on!"

From the stairwell Caliban called: "Is there anything to drink in the house?"

"I don't recognize you! You were never a drinker!" Alain said, opening the apartment door.

"Today's an exception! I want to raise a toast to chastity!" said Caliban as he entered the studio with Charles behind him.

After a moment's hesitation, Alain was debonair again. "If you really want to toast chastity, you have a dream opportunity . . . ," and he waved a hand up at the armoire crowned with the Armagnac bottle.

"Alain, I need to make a phone call," Charles said, and for privacy he vanished into the hallway and closed the door behind him.

Caliban looked at the bottle atop the armoire. "Armagnac!"

"I put it up there so it could reign enthroned like a queen," Alain said.

"What year is it?" Caliban strained to read the label; then said admiringly: "Ah no! Can't be!"

"Open it," Alain commanded. Caliban took a chair and climbed up. But even standing on the chair, he could barely manage to touch the base of the bottle, inaccessible on its proud heights.

The World According to Schopenhauer

Surrounded by those same colleagues at the end of that same long table, Stalin turns to Kalinin: "Believe me, my dear fellow, I too am sure that the city of the renowned Immanuel Kant will remain Kaliningrad forever. As the godfather of his native city, could you please tell us about Kant's most important idea?"

Kalinin hasn't the slightest notion. And so, according to an old habit, tired of their ignorance, Stalin answers his own question:

"Kant's most important idea, comrades, is 'the thing in itself—in German, *das Ding an sich*.' Kant thought that behind our representations there is something objective, a '*Ding*,' that we cannot know but that is real nonetheless. But that idea is wrong. There is nothing real behind our representations, no 'thing in itself,' no *Ding an sich*."

They all listen, bewildered, and Stalin goes on:

"Schopenhauer came closer to the truth. And what, my friends, was Schopenhauer's great idea?"

They all avoid the mocking gaze of the examiner, who, according to a well-known habit, ends by answering the question himself:

"Schopenhauer's great idea, my friends, was that the world is only representation and will. This means that behind the world as we see it before us there is nothing objective, no *Ding an sich*, and that to bring that representation to existence, to make it real, there must be a will, an enormous will that imposes it."

Timidly Zhdanov protests: "Joseph! The world as representation! All your life you've forced us to declare that that was a lie from the idealist philosophy of the bourgeois class!"

Says Stalin: "What, Comrade Zhdanov, is the primary quality of a will?"

Zhdanov is silent, and Stalin answers: "It's freedom. A will can assert whatever it chooses. Let's go on. The real question is this: There are as many different representations of the world as there are individuals on the planet; and inevitably that makes for chaos; how to bring about order in this chaos? The answer is clear: by imposing one single representation on everyone. And the only way to impose it is through one will, one single enormous will, a will that surpasses all other wills. Which I have done, as far as my powers have allowed me. And I assure you that in the grip of a great will, people come to believe anything at all! Oh, friends: anything!" And Stalin laughs, with pleasure in his voice.

Recalling the partridge story, he looks around mischievously at his associates, especially at Khrushchev, short and round; whose cheeks are at that moment flushed red and who dares, once again, to be courageous: "Still, Comrade Stalin, even though people have always believed anything you say, these days they no longer believe you at all."

A Fistfall That Will Be Heard Around the World

"You're right," Stalin answers. "They've stopped believing me. Because my will is weary. My poor will that I totally invested in this daydream that the whole world came to take seriously. I sacrificed all my powers for it, I sacrificed myself. And I ask you to answer this, comrades: Who is it I sacrificed myself for?"

Dazed into silence, the comrades do not even try to open their mouths.

Stalin answers his own question: "I sacrificed myself, comrades, for humanity."

Rather relieved, they all nod approval for the grand words. Kaganovich even goes so far as to applaud.

"But what is humanity? Nothing objective about it, it is only my subjective representation, which is to say: It's what I could see around me with my own eyes. And what did I see with my own eyes, comrades? I saw you—you! Remember the toilets where you would sequester yourselves to rage against my story of the twenty-four partridges! I had a fine time back in the corridor there, listening to you all howling, but at the same time I said to myself: Is it for these fools that I squandered all my powers? Are these the people I lived for? For these imbeciles? For these completely ordinary morons? For these pisspot philosophers? And as I thought about you I felt my will failing, weakening, wearing out, and the dream, our lovely daydream, no longer sustained by my will, collapsed like an enormous building whose beams had been wrecked."

And to illustrate that collapse, Stalin brings his fist down on the table, and it shakes.

The Fall of the Angels

The blow of Stalin's fist resounds in their heads for a long time. Brezhnev looks toward the window and cannot help himself. He cannot believe what he sees: An angel is hanging above the rooftops, its wings spread. He starts up from his seat: "An angel—an angel!"

The others rise too: "An angel? I don't see it!"

"Yes! Up there!"

"Good Lord! Another one! It's falling!" sighs Beria.

"You idiots, you'll be seeing a lot more of them fall," Stalin hisses.

"An angel is a sign!" Khrushchev proclaims.

"A sign? But a sign of what?" moans Brezhnev, paralyzed with fear.

The Old Armagnac Flows over the Floor

Indeed, what is that fall a sign of? A murdered utopia, after which there will never be any other? An era that will leave no trace? Books, paintings, flung into the void? A Europe that will no longer be Europe? Jokes that no one will ever laugh at again?

Alain was not asking himself these questions, frightened as he was at the sight of Caliban, who, grasping the bottle in his hand, had just fallen from the chair onto the floor. He bent over his friend's body, lying on its back and motionless. The only thing moving was the old (oh, the very, very old) Armagnac flowing onto the floor from the broken bottle.

At that moment, at the other end of Paris, a beautiful woman was waking in her bed. She too had heard a blunt, brief sound like a fistfall on a table; behind her closed eyelids, memories of dreams lived on; half-awake, she remembered they were erotic dreams; their specific nature was already hazy, but she felt in a good mood, for without being fascinating or unforgettable, the dreams were unquestionably pleasant.

She heard: "That was very beautiful," and only then did she open her eyes and see a man standing by the door, about to leave. The voice was high-pitched, frail, thin, fragile—like the man himself. Did she know him? Yes; she vaguely remembered a cocktail party at D'Ardelo's where she had also seen old Ramon, who is in love with her; to get away from him she had agreed to leave with a stranger; she remembered that he was very nice, so discreet—nearly invisible—that she could not even recall the moment when they separated downstairs. But, my God, had they separated?

"Really very beautiful, Julie," he repeated from near the door, and she understood, with some surprise, that this man must have spent the night in the same bed with her.

Quaquelique raised a hand for a last good-bye, then went down to the street and sat in his modest car, while in a studio at the other end of Paris, Caliban was picking himself up from the floor with Alain's help.

"Nothing wrong?"

"No, nothing. Everything's all right. Except for the Armagnac—there's none left. I'm sorry, Alain!"

"I'm the one who should apologize," said Alain. "It's my fault for letting you climb onto that old wreck of a chair." Then, concerned: "But, dear fellow, you're limping!"

"A little, but it's not serious."

At that moment, Charles came back from the vestibule and snapped shut his cell phone. He saw Caliban oddly bent over and still holding the broken bottle. "What happened?"

"I broke the bottle," Caliban announced. "There is no more Armagnac. A bad sign."

"Yes, a very bad sign. I have to leave right away for Tarbes," Charles said. "My mother is dying."

When an angel falls, it is certainly a sign. In the
Kremlin meeting room everyone is frightened, staring out the window. Stalin smiles, and—taking advantage of the fact that no one is watching him—he moves
toward an unnoticeable door in a corner. He opens it
and steps into a storage room. There he takes off the
handsome jacket of his official uniform and pulls on a
shabby old parka, then takes up a long hunting rifle.
Thus disguised as a partridge hunter, he steps back
into the room and moves toward the large door onto
the corridor. Everyone is still staring out the win-
dows, and no one sees him. At the last moment, as he
is about to set his hand on the doorknob, he stops for
a second as if to throw one last malicious glance at his
comrades. His eyes meet those of Khrushchev, who
begins to shout:

"It's him! You see him in that outfit? He's trying to
make people think he's a hunter! He's leaving us alone
in this mess! But he's the guilty one! We're all victims!
His victims!"

Stalin is already far down the hallway, and Khrushchev is punching the wall, slamming the table, stomping on the floor with his feet in their huge, badly waxed
Ukrainian boots. He whips the others into a fury
too, and soon they're all shouting, cursing, stamping,

jumping about, pummeling the walls and table with their fists, hammering the floor with their chairs, so that the room reverberates with a hellish sound. It is a riot like earlier ones, when in breaks in the meetings they all gathered in the bathroom in front of the colored urinals decorated with ceramic flowers.

They are all there as before; only Kalinin, quietly, has disappeared. Hounded by a terrible urge to urinate, he wanders through the Kremlin corridors but, unable to find a pissoir anywhere, in the end he runs out into the streets.

PART SEVEN

The Festival of Insignificance

Dialogue on the Motorbike

The next morning, at about eleven, Alain was to meet with his friends Ramon and Caliban in front of the museum near the Luxembourg Gardens. Before he left his studio, he turned back to say good-bye to his mother in the photo. Then he went down to the street and walked toward his motorbike, which was parked not far from his house.

As he straddled the bike, he had the vague sensation of a body leaning against his back. As if Madeleine were with him and touching him lightly.

The illusion moved him; it seemed to express the love he felt for his girl; he started the engine.

Then he heard a voice behind him: "I wanted to talk some more."

No, it wasn't Madeleine; he recognized his mother's voice.

Traffic was slow, and he heard: "I want to be sure there's no confusion between you and me, that we understand each other completely—"

He had to brake. A pedestrian had slipped between cars to cross the street and turned toward Alain with a threatening gesture.

"I'll be frank. I've always felt it's horrible to send a person into the world who didn't ask to be there."

"I know," said Alain.

"Look around you. Of all the people you see, no one is here by his own wish. Of course, what I just said is the most banal truth there is. So banal, and so basic, that we've stopped seeing it and hearing it."

For several minutes he kept to a lane between a truck and a car that were pressing him from either side.

"Everyone jabbers about human rights. What a joke! Your existence isn't founded on any right. They don't even allow you to end your life by your own choice, these defenders of human rights."

The light at the intersection went red. He stopped. Pedestrians from both sides of the street set out toward the opposite sidewalk.

And the mother went on: "Look at them all! Look! At least half the people you're seeing are ugly. Being ugly—is that one of the human rights too? And do you know what it is to carry your ugliness along through your whole life? With not a moment of relief? Or your sex—you never chose that. Or the color of your eyes. Or your era on earth. Or your country. Or your mother. None of the things that matter. The rights a person can have involve only pointless things, for which there is no reason to fight, or to write great declarations!"

He was driving again now, and his mother's voice grew gentler. "You're here as you are because I was weak. That was my fault. Forgive me."

Alain was silent; then he said in a quiet voice: "What is it you feel guilty for? For not having the strength to prevent my birth? Or for not reconciling yourself to my life, which, as it happens, is actually not so bad?"

After a silence, she answered: "Maybe you're right. Then I'm doubly guilty."

"I'm the one who should apologize," said Alain. "I dropped into your life like a cow turd. I chased you away to America."

"Quit your apologies! What do you know about my life, my little idiot! Can I call you idiot? Yes, don't be angry; in my opinion you are an idiot! And you know where your idiocy comes from? From your goodness! Your ridiculous goodness!"

He reached the Luxembourg Gardens. He parked the bike.

"Don't protest, and let me apologize," he said. "I'm an apologizer. That's the way you made me, you and he. And as such, as an apologizer, I'm happy. I feel good when we apologize to each other, you and I. Isn't it lovely, apologizing to each other?"

Then they walked toward the museum:

"Believe me," he said, "I agree with everything you've just said. With everything. Isn't it lovely to be in agreement, you and me? Isn't it lovely, our alliance?"

"Alain! Alain!" A man's voice interrupted their conversation. "You're looking at me as if you never saw me before!"

Ramon Talks with Alain About the Age of the Navel

Yes, it was Ramon. "This morning Caliban's wife phoned," he told Alain. "She told me about last night. I know everything. Charles has gone to Tarbes. His mother is dying."

"I know," said Alain. "And Caliban? When he was at my house he fell off a chair."

"She told me. And it wasn't so trivial. She says he's having trouble walking. He's in pain. Now he's sleeping. He wanted to see the Chagall show with us, and he won't see it."

"Neither will I, actually. I cannot bear waiting in line. Look!"

He waved toward the crowd moving slowly toward the museum door.

"It's not so long, the line," said Alain.

"Not so long, but disgusting anyhow."

"How many times is it now that you've come and left?"

"Three times. So that, really, I don't come here to see Chagall but to take note that from one week to the next the lines are longer and longer, thus that the planet is more and more heavily populated. Look at them! You think that suddenly they all started to love Chagall? They'll go anywhere, do anything, just to kill time they don't know what to do with. They don't know anything, so they let themselves be led around. They're superbly leadable. Excuse me. I'm in a foul mood. Yesterday I drank a lot. I really did drink too much."

"So then what do you want to do?"

"Let's walk in the park! It's nice weather. I know, Sundays it's a little more crowded. But it's fine. Look! The sun!"

Alain did not object. True, the atmosphere in the park was peaceful. There were people running, there were passersby, on the lawn there were rings of people going through strange, slow motions, there were people eating ice cream; inside the enclosures there were people playing tennis.

"I feel better here," said Ramon. "Of course, uniformity rules everywhere. But in this park it has a wider choice of uniforms. So you can hold on to the illusion of your own individuality."

"The illusion of individuality . . . It's odd: A few minutes ago I had a strange conversation."

"A conversation? With whom?"

"And then the navel—"

"What navel?"

"I haven't talked to you about that? For a while now I've been thinking a lot about navels . . ."

As if some invisible theater director had arranged it, two very young girls walked by, their navels elegantly exposed.

Ramon could only say: "There we are."

And Alain: "Walking around with the navel uncovered is the fashion now. It has been for at least ten years."

"It will pass, like any other fashion."

"But don't forget that the navel fashion came in with the new century! As if on that symbolic date someone raised the blinds that, for centuries, had kept us from seeing the essential thing: that individuality is an illusion!"

"Yes, that's indubitable, but what has it to do with the navel?"

"On woman's erotic body there are certain golden sites: I always thought there were three such: the thighs, the buttocks, the breasts."

Ramon considered, and: "All right," he said.

"Then one day I understood that there is a fourth: the navel."

After a moment's reflection, Ramon agreed: "Yes. Maybe."

And Alain: "The thighs, the breasts, the buttocks have a different shape on each woman. So those three golden sites are not only arousing, they also express a woman's individuality. You could never mistake the buttocks of the woman you love. The beloved buttocks, you'd recognize them among a hundred others. But you could not identify the woman you love by her navel. All navels are alike."

At least twenty children, laughing and shouting, ran past the two friends.

Alain went on: "Each of those four golden sites represents an erotic message. And I wonder what erotic message the navel tells us." After a pause: "One thing is obvious: Unlike the thighs, the buttocks, or the breasts, the navel says nothing about the woman bearing it; it speaks of something which is not that woman."

"What then?"

"The fetus."

"Yes, of course, the fetus," Ramon agreed.

Alain again: "In the past, love was the celebration of the individual, of the inimitable, the tribute to a unique thing, a thing impossible to replicate. But not only does the navel not revolt against repetition, it is a call for repetitions! And in our millennium we are going to live under the sign of the navel. Under that sign we are all, every one of us, the soldiers of sex: all of us setting our sights not on the beloved woman but on the same small hole in the middle of the belly, the hole that represents the sole meaning, the sole goal, the sole future of all erotic desire."

Suddenly an unexpected arrival interrupted the conversation. There before them, approaching along the same pathway, was D'Ardelo.

The Arrival of D'Ardelo

He too had drunk a good deal, had slept poorly, and was now out to clear his head with a walk in the Luxembourg Gardens. The sight of Ramon made him uncomfortable at first. He had only invited the man to his cocktail party as a courtesy, since Ramon had found him two good servers for the event. But since this retiree was no longer important to him, D'Ardelo had not even looked for a moment to greet him and bid him welcome to the gathering. Now, feeling guilty, he spread his arms wide and cried, "Ramon! My friend!"

Ramon remembered slipping away from the party without even saying a simple good-bye to his old colleague. But D'Ardelo's hearty greeting now relieved his bad conscience; he too threw wide his arms, cried,

"Hello there, friend!" introduced Alain, and cordially invited the newcomer to join them.

D'Ardelo well remembered that it was in this very park that some sudden inspiration had caused him to invent the bizarre lie about his mortal illness. What to do now? He couldn't contradict himself; he could only go on being gravely ill; actually, he did not find it much of a problem, having quickly understood that there was no need to restrain his good mood on that account, for cheerful banter makes a tragically ill man all the more appealing and admirable.

So in a light, amusing tone he went on chatting to Ramon and his friend about the gardens as a piece of his own highly personal landscape, his "countryside," as he called it several times; he expanded on all the statues of poets, painters, statesmen, kings: "You see how the France of the past is still alive!" then, with a light playful irony, he pointed to the white statues of the great ladies of France—queens, princesses, regents—each standing on a tall plinth, in all her grandeur from foot to head; each separated from the next by some ten or fifteen yards, together they formed a very large ring overlooking a pretty stone pool below.

Farther off, very noisily, children were arriving in groups from different directions and gathering together.

"Ah, the children! You hear them laughing?" D'Ardelo smiled.

"There's a holiday today, I forget what . . . some special children's day, whatever."

Suddenly he snapped to attention: "But what's going on over there?"

A Hunter and a Pisser Arrive

In the broad walk that stretches into the park from l'avenue de l'Observatoire, a man of about fifty with a mustache, wearing an old worn parka with a long hunting rifle slung from his shoulder, runs toward the circle of the great marble ladies of France. He is shouting and waving his arms. All around, people stop and watch, startled and sympathetic. Yes, sympathetic, for that mustachioed face has an easy quality that freshens the atmosphere in the garden with an idyllic breath of times gone by. It calls up the image of a ladies' man, a village rake, an adventurer who's the more likable for already being a little older and seasoned. Won over by his country charm, his virile goodness, his folkloric look, the crowd sends him smiles and he responds, pleased and ingratiating.

Then, still at a run, he raises a hand toward one of the statues. Everyone looks that way and sees another man—a very old one, painfully thin, with a little pointed goatee—who, hoping to protect himself from prying eyes, ducks behind the bulky pedestal of a marble great lady.

"Look, look!" the hunter says, and setting his rifle on his shoulder he fires toward the statue. This one is Marie de Médicis, Queen of France, known for her old, heavy, ugly, arrogant face. The gunshot blows off her nose, so that she looks even older, uglier, heavier, more arrogant, while the old man hiding behind her pedestal sets off running still farther away, terrified, and hoping to escape the prying eyes, he ends up crouching behind Valentine de Milan, Duchess of Orléans (who is much more beautiful).

The people are disconcerted by the unexpected rifle shot and by Marie de Médicis' face stripped of a nose; uncertain how to react, they look to left and right, seeking some sign that will enlighten them: What to make of the hunter's behavior? Should they see him as blameworthy or playful? Should they hiss him or applaud him?

As if he sensed their discomfort, the hunter cries:

"Pissing in the most famous French park—that's forbidden!" Then, looking around at his small audience, he bursts into laughter, and his laugh is so gay, so free, so innocent, so rustic, so brotherly, so contagious that everyone around, as if relieved, starts laughing as well.

The old man with the pointy goatee comes out from behind the statue of the queen of Brittany buttoning his fly; his face beaming with the contentment of relief.

On Ramon's face a good mood appears. "Doesn't that hunter remind you of something?" he asks Alain.

"Yes, he does: Charles."

"Yes. Charles is here with us. It's the last act of his theater piece."

The Festival of Insignificance

Meanwhile, some fifty children have pulled away from the crowd and formed a half circle like a chorus. Alain takes a few steps toward them, curious to see what will happen, and D'Ardelo says to Ramon: "See, the performances here are excellent. Those two characters are perfect! They must be actors between jobs. Unemployed fellows. Look! They don't need a theater stage. The pathways of a park are enough for them. They don't give up their calling. They want to keep active. They're struggling to live." Then he remembers his serious illness and, to call to mind his tragic destiny, he adds in a lower voice: "I'm struggling too."

"I know, friend, and I admire your courage," says Ramon and, with the intent to support him in his misfortune, he adds: "For a long while now, D'Ardelo,

I've wanted to talk to you about something. About the value of insignificance. In the past I was mainly thinking about your relations with women. I wanted to tell you about Quaquelique. My great friend Quaquelique. You don't know him, I know. Never mind. At this point, though, insignificance looks entirely different to me than it did back then; I see it in a whole other way—in a stronger, more revealing light. Insignificance, my friend, is the essence of existence. It is all around us, and everywhere and always. It is present even when no one wants to see it: in horror, in bloody battles, in the worst disasters. It often takes courage to acknowledge it in such dramatic situations, and to call it by name. But it is not only a matter of acknowledging it, we must love insignificance, we must learn to love it. Right here, in this park, before us—look, my friend, it is present here in all its obviousness, all its innocence, in all its beauty. Yes, its beauty. As you yourself said: the perfect performance . . . and utterly useless, the children laughing . . . without knowing why—isn't that beautiful? Breathe, D'Ardelo, my friend, inhale this insignificance that's all around us, it is the key to wisdom, it is the key to a good mood . . ."

Just then, a few yards in front of them, the man with the mustache takes the old man with the goatee by his shoulders and speaks to the people gathered around them in words he pronounces in a fine, solemn voice: "Comrades! My old friend here has sworn on his honor that he will never again piss on the great ladies of France!"

Then, once again, he explodes with laughter, the crowd applauds and shouts, and the mother says, "Alain, I'm happy to be here with you." Then her voice turns into a light, calm, gentle laugh.

"You're laughing?" says Alain, for this is the first time he is hearing his mother's laughter.

"Yes."

"I'm happy too," he says, with emotion.

D'Ardelo, on the other hand, says nothing, and Ramon understands that his hymn to insignificance has not succeeded in pleasing this man so attached to the gravity of grand truths; he decides to go about it differently:

"I saw you yesterday, La Franck and you. You were beautiful, together."

He watches D'Ardelo's face and sees that this time his words are far better received. This success inspires him, and an idea suddenly occurs to him, the idea of a lie as absurd as it is ravishing, which he decides forthwith to turn into a gift, a gift to a man who hasn't much longer to live.

"But be careful—if anyone sees you, things are all too clear!"

"Clear? What?" asks D'Ardelo, with barely concealed pleasure.

"Clear that you're lovers. No, don't deny it, I

understood it all. And don't worry, there isn't a man on earth more discreet than I am."

D'Ardelo looks deep into Ramon's eyes, where, as in a mirror, he sees the reflection of a man tragically ill and yet happy, the companion of a famous woman he has never touched and of whom he has become, in an instant, the secret lover.

"My friend," he says, and he clasps Ramon in his arms. Then, his eyes moist, he leaves, happy and light-hearted.

The children's chorus has already formed a perfect half circle and their conductor, a boy of ten dressed in a tuxedo, baton in hand, prepares to give the signal for the concert to begin.

But he must wait a few moments, for a little carriage painted red and yellow, drawn by two ponies, comes clattering up. The mustachioed man in his worn parka raises his long shotgun. The coachman, a child himself, obeys, and stops the carriage. The mustachioed fellow and the old man with the goatee climb in, sit down, send a last salute to the audience, who wave their arms in delight while the children's chorus begins singing "La Marseillaise."

The little carriage sets off, and along a broad pathway leaves the Luxembourg Gardens and disappears slowly into the Paris streets.

The Franco-Czech novelist Milan Kundera was born in Brno and has lived in France, his second homeland, since 1975. He is the author of the novels *The Joke, Life Is Elsewhere, Farewell Waltz, The Book of Laughter and Forgetting, The Unbearable Lightness of Being*, and *Immortality*, and the short story collection *Laughable Loves*—all originally in Czech. His more recent novels, *Slowness, Identity*, and *Ignorance*, as well as his nonfiction works, *The Art of the Novel, Testaments Betrayed, The Curtain*, and *Encounter*, were originally written in French.